THE GREAT SHABBOS FOOD DEBATE

by Rabbi B.

Illustrated by Nechama Leibler

ISRAEL BOOKSHOP
Publications

About the author:

Yossi Berktin, fondly known as Rabbi B., is a Toronto-based children's musician and entertainer. He has been educating, performing, and entertaining young children for many years, and loves telling stories. For more of his work, please visit his website at rabbibmusic.blogspot.ca. To book or speak with Rabbi B., please email him at rabbibmusic@gmail.com.

Published by:
Israel Bookshop Publications
501 Prospect Street
Lakewood, NJ 08701
Tel: (732) 901-3009 / Fax: (732) 901-4012
www.israelbookshoppublications.com
info@israelbookshoppublications.com

Printed in The United States of America

Distributed in Israel by:
Shanky's
Petach Tikva 16
Jerusalem
972-2-538-6936

Distributed in Australia by:
Gold's Book and Gift Company
3-13 William Street
Balaclava 3183
613-9527-8775

Distributed in Europe by:
Lehmanns
Unit E Viking Industrial Park
Rolling Mill Road
Jarrow, Tyne & Wear NE32 3DP
44-191-430-0333

Distributed in South Africa by:
Kollel Bookshop
Northfield Centre
17 Northfield Avenue
Glenhazel 2192
27-11-440-6679

This book is
dedicated to
Kayla, Menachem
Mendel, and Eli,
the first Rabbi B. fans!

There's a grocery store, down on Shalom Way,
Where people come shop, day after day.
But after store hours, when darkness comes in,
A call can be heard: "Okay, let's begin!"

Then all of the items that sell in the store,
Which stood oh-so-silently still before,
Begin to wake up, to discuss and to speak
About the events of that day and that week.

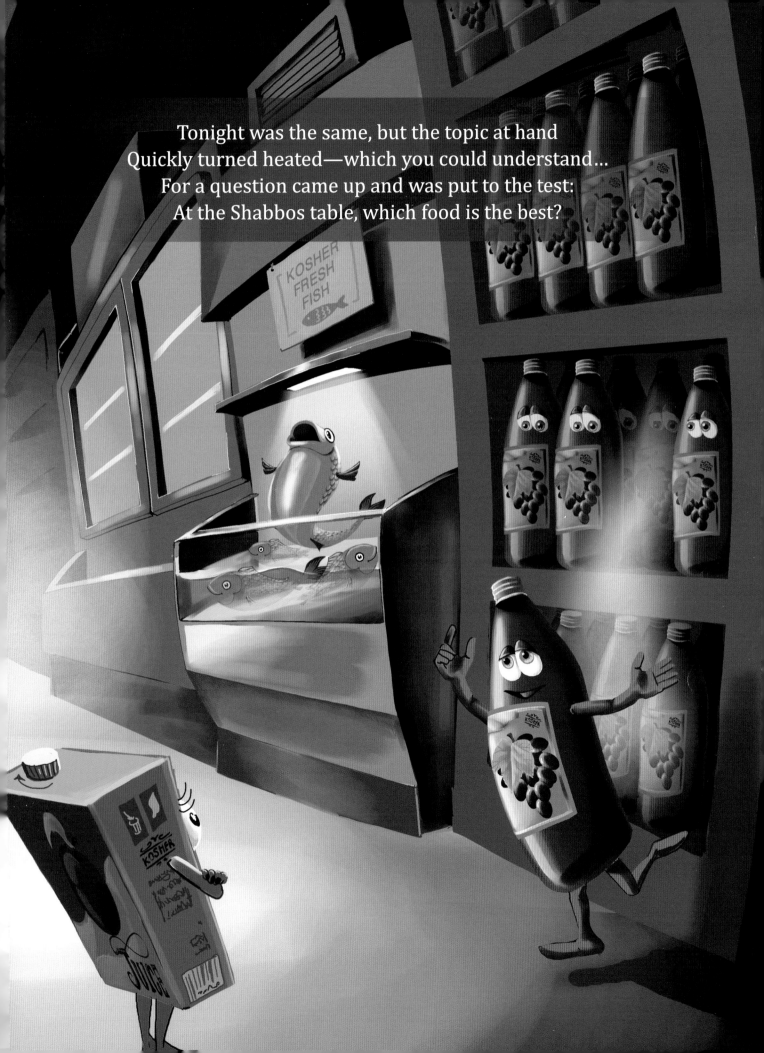

Tonight was the same, but the topic at hand
Quickly turned heated—which you could understand...
For a question came up and was put to the test:
At the Shabbos table, which food is the best?

The wine bottle went first, from high on the shelf;
It sure had a lot to say 'bout itself.
"I'm used for Kiddush, at each Shabbos meal,
And look at how happy I make people feel!

"They drink me and then they break out in a grin…
I'm surely the greatest; I will always win!
That makes me the best, though I don't mean to boast;
For Shabbos it's *me* the people like most."

Next to be heard was the warm challah bread.
It spoke of its greatness, and here's what it said:
"I'm not sold alone; challah goes out in pairs.
It's the challah about which everyone cares.

"I'm soft and delicious, a real Shabbos treat;
A *seudah* without me would not be complete.
That makes me the best, though I don't mean to boast;
For Shabbos it's *me* the people like most."

"You are quite mistaken," said a fish, freshly caught.
"I'm the best food that can ever be bought.
I'm found in the Torah, with my fins and my scales;
Yes, I'm the one who drives up the sales.

"I'm the first course at the meal Friday night;
In one slice of gefilte you'll find much delight.
That makes me the best, though I don't mean to boast;
For Shabbos it's *me* the people like most."

Splish, splash, went the soup as it raised up its voice.
"No, no, *I'm* the one which is the best choice!
I'm served to each person, all get their own bowl,
And I warm those who eat me, both in body and soul.

"I can cure common colds, and soothe a sore throat;
Put in a *kneidel*, or croutons that float.
That makes me the best, though I don't mean to boast;
For Shabbos it's *me* the people like most."

Then from the fridge something proudly declared,
"You think that to me you can all be compared?
I am the chicken—I'm the main meal!
I make the *seudah*, yes, I'm the best deal!

"You can spice, dress, and cook me in any which way;
Eat me Friday night, and again Shabbos day.
That makes me the best, though I don't mean to boast;
For Shabbos it's *me* the people like most."

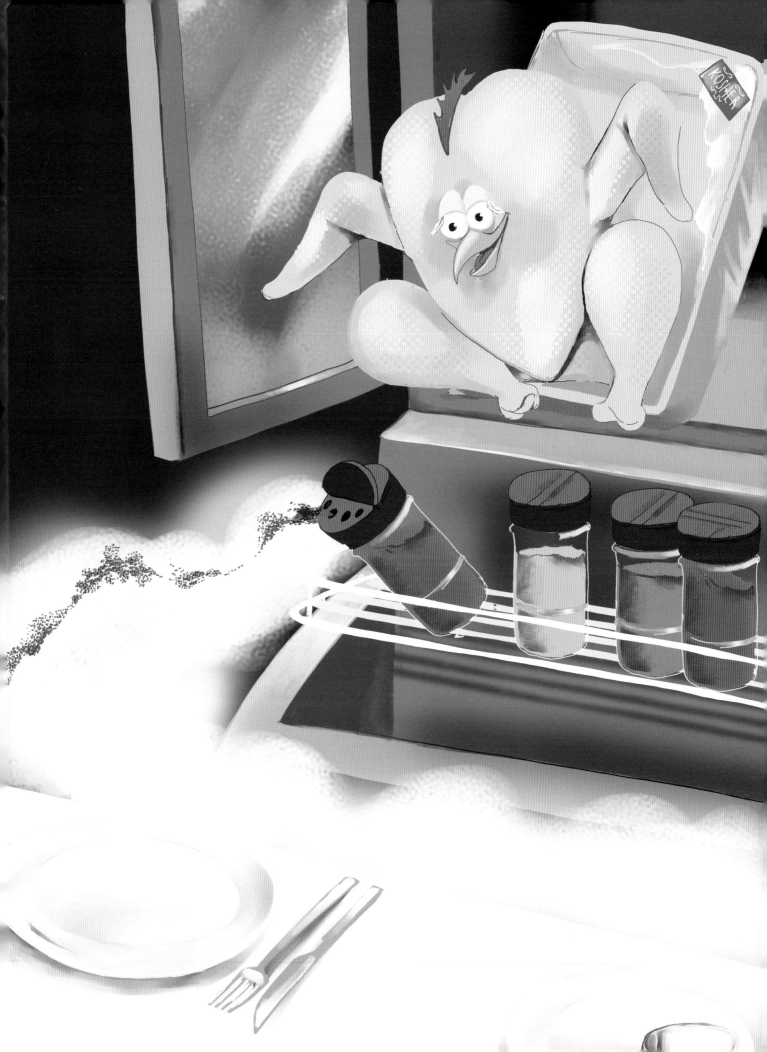

"Wait just a minute!" said a voice from the shelf.
"I'm the high point of the meal by myself!
I'm chocolate cake, and I'm simply the best;
When I'm on the table, there is no contest.

"I'm thick and I'm gooey and I'm simply adored;
Before I appear, the people are bored.
That makes me the best, though I don't mean to boast;
For Shabbos it's *me* the people like most."

The debate continued all through that night,
Until finally came morning with the sun's early light.
In walked a smiling boy, a list in his hand.
To shop for his mother was what he had planned.

The Shabbos foods needed, he read line by line:
Challah, fish, soup, chicken, a cake, and some wine.
The boy took them all, and then went to pay...
And the foods in his bag did not know what to say.

Now who was best? Which did he most need?
In their hearts they all knew, and they all agreed,
That *each food* was special and would have its own place
At the table of the boy with the smile on his face.

The boy and his family sat down Friday night
For their Shabbos meal, in the warm candlelight.
The foods looked around and knew each was best.
Each one was important; each one was blessed.